A Note to Parents and Caregivers:

Read-it! Readers are for children who are just starting on the amazing road to reading. These beautiful books support both the acquisition of reading skills and the love of books.

The PURPLE LEVEL presents basic topics and objects using high frequency words and simple language patterns.

The RED LEVEL presents familiar topics using common words and repeating sentence patterns.

The BLUE LEVEL presents new ideas using a larger vocabulary and varied sentence structure.

The YELLOW LEVEL presents more challenging ideas, a broad vocabulary, and wide variety in sentence structure.

The GREEN LEVEL presents more complex ideas, an extended vocabulary range, and expanded language structures.

The ORANGE LEVEL presents a wide range of ideas and concepts using challenging vocabulary and complex language structures.

When sharing a book with your child, read in short stretches, pausing often to talk about the pictures. Have your child turn the pages and point to the pictures and familiar words. And be sure to reread favorite stories or parts of stories.

There is no right or wrong way to share books with children. Find time to read with your child, and pass on the legacy of literacy.

Adria F. Klein, Ph.D.
Professor Emeritus
California State University
San Bernardino, California

Editor: Jill Kalz
Designer: Nathan Gassman
Page Production: Amy Muehlenhardt
Creative Director: Keith Griffin
Editorial Director: Carol Jones
The illustrations in this book were created with watercolor.

Picture Window Books
5115 Excelsior Boulevard
Suite 232
Minneapolis, MN 55416
877-845-8392
www.picturewindowbooks.com

Printed in the United States of America.

Library of Congress Cataloging-in-Publication Data
Williams, Jacklyn.
Welcome to third grade, Gus! / by Jacklyn Williams ; illustrated by Doug Cushman.
p. cm. — (Read-it! readers. Gus the hedgehog)
Summary: On the first day of third grade, Gus worries that his teacher will be a
monster, his classmates will call him names, and it will be the worst day of his life,
but when it is over he discovers that most of his fears were unfounded.
ISBN-13: 978-1-4048-2714-1 (hardcover)
ISBN-10: 1-4048-2714-5 (hardcover)
[1. First day of school—Fiction. 2. Worry—Fiction. 3. Schools—Fiction.
4. Hedgehogs—Fiction.] I. Cushman, Doug, ill. II. Title. III. Series.
PZ7.W6656Wel 2006
[E]—dc22   2006003384

Welcome to Third Grade, Gus!

by Jacklyn Williams
illustrated by Doug Cushman

Special thanks to our advisers for their expertise:

Adria F. Klein, Ph.D.
Professor Emeritus, California State University
San Bernardino, California

Susan Kesselring, M.A.
Literacy Educator
Rosemount–Apple Valley–Eagan (Minnesota) School District

PICTURE WINDOW BOOKS
Minneapolis, Minnesota

The teacher held out her scaly green hand.
She pointed at Gus with one long, sharp claw.

"Welcome to third grade, Gussss, Gussss,
Gussss," she hissed.

Gus screamed and opened his eyes. "It was only a dream," he told himself.

Gus' mom poked her head through the doorway. "Time to get ready for school, Gus," she said.

"I'm not going," Gus said, pulling the covers over his head.

"Third grade is a hard, scary, no-fun place," he continued.

"How do you know?" asked his mom. "You've never been to third grade. Now, hurry up, or you'll miss the bus."

Gus wiggled out of his pajamas and into his new school clothes. After breakfast, he grabbed his new lunch box and followed his mom out the door.

Halfway to the bus stop, Gus started to rub his stomach. "I think I'm sick," he said.

"Don't be scared," said his mom. "You'll feel much better when you get to school."

Gus climbed on the bus and slid onto the seat beside Bean. "I'll never have another day of fun as long as I live," Gus sighed.

Just when Gus thought things couldn't get any worse, Billy Dixon plopped down on the seat behind him.

Gus leaned close to Bean. "I'm worried," he whispered.

"About what?" asked Bean.

"About everything," said Gus. "Especially third grade."

"I think you worry too much," said Bean.

"Do you think the teacher will yell?" Gus asked. "Do you think she'll make us stand in the corner for an hour?"

Billy poked his head over the seat. "She'll yell all right," he said. "A LOT! And you'll be in the corner FOR DAYS!"

The bus pulled up in front of the school.
Bean got off. Gus trailed behind him.

"Number forty-two, number forty-two,"
Gus mumbled, trying to remember which
bus would take him home again.

When they reached the front door, Bean
looked around. Gus was nowhere to be seen.

"Psst, Bean," said a voice from behind a bush.
"I'm going to wait here. Come by and get me
after school."

"Come on, Gus," said Bean. "Everything is going to be OK. You worry too much."

"But what if I say something dumb in front of the whole class?" Gus asked. "What if they call me 'Spike Head'? What if the teacher yells a lot and makes us stand in the corner for days? You heard what Billy said."

"Don't listen to Billy," said Bean. "He is just trying to scare you. Third grade will be just as much fun as second grade was."

Gus and Bean made their way through the crowded hallway. Children bustled this way and that. Then the bell rang, and everyone disappeared.

By the time Gus and Bean found their classroom, all of the other children were in their seats.

"It looks like I have one less thing to worry about," Gus whispered to Bean. "Billy isn't in our class."

Then Gus' heart skipped a beat. The only two
empty desks were in the front row. And right
in front of them stood ... THE TEACHER!

Bean gave Gus a nudge. "Go on," he said.

With shaky knees, Gus slunk to the first desk and sat down.

"Good morning, class," said the teacher.
"I'm Mrs. Kyle. Welcome to third grade."

Mrs. Kyle leaned over to Gus. She whispered in a soft, gentle voice, "Don't worry. Everyone is nervous the first day, even me."

She smiled a great, big, non-scary smile. She didn't have huge fangs, long claws, or scaly green skin.

Gus spent the rest of the day having so much fun that he forgot to worry. First, the class played a game to learn each other's names. No one called Gus "Spike Head."

Then Mrs. Kyle asked everyone to choose a partner for a science project. Three kids begged Gus to be their partner.

At recess, Gus caught a fly ball. At lunch, he dropped his cookie, but the cafeteria lady gave him another one. And after music class, Mrs. Kyle chose him to put away the drums.

At last, the bell rang. It was time to go home. Gus had been having so much fun all day that he had forgotten to go to the bathroom. He started to squirm.

"Before you leave," said Mrs. Kyle, "I have one more thing to tell you."

As Mrs. Kyle talked, Gus began to jiggle his feet. He wiggled his legs. He wriggled and rocked back and forth.

Finally, Mrs. Kyle said, "Class dismissed!"

The door burst open. Children poured out.
At the head of the mob ran Gus.

Bean ran to catch up.

"Where are you going?" he asked.

Gus slid to a stop in front of the bathrooms.

"You know what, Bean?" Gus said. "Third grade isn't a hard, scary, no-fun place after all. Today was fun. I can't wait until tomorrow! See you on bus forty-two!"

"But, Gus," Bean said, "I think that's—"

"Trust me. It's bus forty-two," said Gus. "I think you worry too much, Bean!"

More *Read-it!* Readers

Bright pictures and fun stories help you practice your reading skills. Look for more books at your level.

Happy Birthday, Gus! 1-4048-0957-0

Happy Easter, Gus! 1-4048-0959-7

Happy Halloween, Gus! 1-4048-0960-0

Happy Thanksgiving, Gus! 1-4048-0961-9

Happy Valentine's Day, Gus! 1-4048-0962-7

Let's Go Fishing, Gus! 1-4048-2713-7

Make a New Friend, Gus! 1-4048-2711-0

Matt Goes to Mars 1-4048-1269-5

Merry Christmas, Gus! 1-4048-0958-9

Pick a Pet, Gus! 1-4048-2712-9

Rumble Meets Buddy Beaver 1-4048-1287-3

Rumble Meets Chester the Chef 1-4048-1335-7

Rumble Meets Eli Elephant 1-4048-1332-2

Rumble Meets Keesha Kangaroo 1-4048-1290-3

Rumble Meets Milly the Maid 1-4048-1341-1

Rumble Meets Penny Panther 1-4048-1331-4

Rumble Meets Sylvia and Sally Swan 1-4048-1541-4

Rumble Meets Wally Warthog 1-4048-1289-X

Looking for a specific title or level? A complete list of *Read-it!* Readers is available on our Web site:
www.picturewindowbooks.com